# Little Archie and the Spectacular Disaster-Magnet TV Gadget

Other Little Archie adventures by Miles Gibson and Neal Layton

# Little Archie

**Mil**

in a seaside town on the edge of the New Forest. An author of adult fiction and poetry, he is also a screenwriter and artist. When Miles was little, his grandfather used to do clever conjuring tricks – but he never invented a TV quite like Uncle Bernie's.

**Neal Layton** studied Illustration at Saint Martins School of Art. He has won and been shortlisted for the prestigious Nestlé Prize several times and his distinctive artwork features in many award-winning children's fiction and picture books. Neal lives with his girlfriend and a collection of nodding-dog toys.

# Little Archie and the Spectacular Disaster-Magnet TV Gadget

Miles Gibson

Illustrated by Neal Layton

MACMILLAN CHILDREN'S BOOKS

First published 2006 as *Whoops – There Goes Joe!*
by Macmillan Children's Books

This edition published 2008 by Macmillan Children's Books
a division of Macmillan Publishers Limited
20 New Wharf Road, London N1 9RR
Basingstoke and Oxford
www.panmacmillan.com

Associated companies throughout the world

ISBN: 978-0-330-44779-9



1 3 5 7 9 8 6 4 2

A CIP catalogue record for this book is available from
the British Library.

Printed and bound in Great Britain by Mackays of Chatham plc, Kent

**For Susan**
**M.G.**

**For Tommy Griffin**
**N.L.**

# Chapter 1

Archie Bodkin lived with his mother and father in a small house in the big city. He had a goldfish and a baby brother. He called the goldfish Bodger. The name of his baby brother was Joe.

Archie led a regular life. He had regular baths and regularly combed his hair, owned a regulation lunch box and regularly went to school.

"You have to stay regular," said his mother and father, who made a habit of giving people good advice.

Archie was as regular as clockwork. Every evening, after homework, he liked to sit down

to watch TV. He watched *Captain Marvellous in Space* and programmes containing animals. They were his regular favourites.

Joe – who was only two years old – watched anything he could find by flicking through the channels with the remote control.

He liked all the cartoons, picture puzzles, adventures and comedies.

But magic shows starring Cyril the Clown were his particular favourites. Almost everyone agreed that Baby Joe watched too much TV.

The trouble began one day when Uncle Bernie paid a visit. Uncle Bernie lived in a house called the Jackdaw's Nest. He had a nose like a raspberry and whiskers sprouting from his ears. He lived with a telescope, a parrot and many gadgets of his own invention. He'd invented a talking toaster that shouted at you when the toast was

done, a rocket-propelled skateboard and a pair of luminous slippers that were easier to find if you had to get out of bed in the dark.

Archie loved Uncle Bernie. But his mother and father disapproved of him.

"He's a bad influence on the boy," they used to tell each other sadly. "His inventions are extremely odd and he doesn't keep regular hours."

# Chapter 2

The day the trouble began, Uncle Bernie arrived at the house with a special surprise for the family.

"What is it?" asked Archie as they watched Uncle Bernie struggling

through the front door. He was pulling an enormous parcel made from cardboard and held together with tape and string.

"It's a television," said Uncle Bernie proudly as he unwrapped a strange contraption with lots of dials and buttons and a screen the size of a wardrobe door.

The Bodkins looked puzzled.

"We already have a television," explained Mr Bodkin.

Uncle Bernie laughed. "Yes, but this is one of my own invention. It has extra grommets and gizmos and plenty of whatsits and thingamajigs. It has an egg timer and a radio, a thermometer and an alarm clock. It has everything."

"It's certainly big," said Archie.

"Yes," said Uncle Bernie. "And it has two hundred channels. It's very educational."

Archie's mother and father looked

doubtful. But they couldn't refuse a gift that was very educational.

"I'll show you how it works," Uncle Bernie told Archie. "Look. I've made a special remote control." He pulled a black plastic box from his pocket. The box was studded with lots of buttons.

"You press the top buttons – red, blue and orange – to change the channels. And the middle buttons – purple, green and yellow – to select the language. And the bottom buttons – russet, rose and lavender – to control the colour, contrast and volume."

He pressed several buttons and the television crackled and popped and glowed with a brilliant light. They saw a lady explaining in Swedish how to make a sponge cake.

Uncle Bernie changed the channel with his special gadget. The sponge-cake lady disappeared and they saw a man in a yellow bow tie, talking about the ruins of Rome.

"That's very educational," agreed Mr and Mrs Bodkin.

"Yes," said Uncle Bernie. "I hope it gives you hours of pleasure." And he laughed as he hurried away, back to the Jackdaw's Nest in time to feed the parrot.

*

For the first few days they watched everything they could find on their new television. They watched classical dancing in Darjeeling and juggling in Japan. They watched traffic news from Trinidad, the weather forecast for Florida and a history of Halifax, Nova Scotia. And then they grew tired of the novelty and went back to watching their regular programmes.

By the end of the week they had all stopped spending so much time sitting in front of Uncle Bernie's

contraption

. . . except for

Baby Joe.

Baby Joe just

couldn't stop.

Whenever Archie came home from school he'd find Baby Joe sitting on the floor watching the TV with his nose pressed against the enormous screen and his fingers playing with the buttons on the remote control.

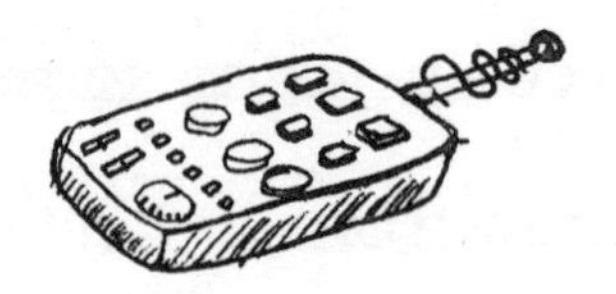

# Chapter 3

“Come and play with me,” Archie said to Joe one Saturday afternoon. “There are caterpillars in the garden.” He was searching for his magnifying glass in the cupboard.

Baby Joe looked at Archie and grinned. He liked caterpillars. But he shook his head. He was watching television.

Archie went into the garden when their mother came into the room. She looked at Baby Joe and said, "Come into the kitchen. I'll make you some strawberry milk."

Joe looked up at his mother and grinned. He liked strawberry milk. But he shook his head. He was watching television.

Mrs Bodkin went back to the kitchen, where Mr Bodkin was eating a sandwich. "I'm worried about our baby," she said. "He watches too much TV."

"Everyone likes TV," said Mr Bodkin, brushing crumbs from his cardigan. He still liked to watch the football on Wednesday nights and he knew his wife enjoyed watching people gardening on a Sunday afternoon. There was nothing wrong with that. He couldn't see the harm in it.

"But Joe is just a baby. When he grows up he'll have square eyes. It can't be healthy. I think you should talk to him."

Mr Bodkin sighed, wiped the butter from his moustache and walked into the living room.

Joe was still sitting on the floor watching TV with his nose pressed against the screen.

"Hello," said Mr Bodkin. "Would you like me to read you a story?"

Joe looked up at his father and grinned. He liked his father reading stories. But he shook his head. He was watching television.

Mr Bodkin frowned.

"If you sit too close to the screen, one day the TV will swallow you up," he warned. And he scooped Joe from the floor and put him beneath his arm.

"We'll sit together," said Mr Bodkin as he found a book and settled down in his favourite armchair. He placed Joe beside him in the cushions and began to read him a story.

But it was a warm afternoon and Mr Bodkin – who had eaten several sandwiches – yawned and fell asleep. He began to snore, and the storybook fell from his hand.

Baby Joe was soon feeling bored and uncomfortable. He wriggled and squirmed. He climbed down from the chair and crawled back to the big TV set. He clapped his hands in delight at the grommets and gizmos; blew bubbles at the whatsits and thingamajigs.

He looked at the screen, where a walrus was dancing with a polar bear. The bear wore a pair of spectacles. The walrus was waving a bowler hat.

Joe sat on the carpet and stared. "Woo-woo!" he said to the walrus. "Woo-woo!"

He pressed his hands against the screen and laughed. "Boo-boo!" he said to the bear. "Boo-boo!"

Then he picked up Uncle Bernie's special remote control and started to play with the buttons. There was a crackle and a flash and a loud whoosh – and then nothing at all but the sound of Mr Bodkin snoring . . .

# Chapter 4

"Where's Joe?" said Archie when he came back from the garden after looking at caterpillars through his magnifying glass. He stared around the room, but Baby Joe was nowhere to be seen.

Mr Bodkin woke up with a snort and Mrs Bodkin gave a shriek and came

running from the kitchen. "What ßhave you done with our baby?" she demanded, frowning at her husband.

"He was sitting here a minute ago," complained Mr Bodkin. He stood up and glared at the chair, as if he thought it might be playing stupid

tricks on him and hiding the baby behind its cushions.

"I can't leave you alone for five minutes," said Mrs Bodkin.

"Look!" said Archie.

"What?" cried Mrs Bodkin.

"There!" said Archie.

"Where?" shouted Mr Bodkin.

"He's inside the TV set!"

At first they didn't believe it. They gathered very close around the enormous screen and stared.

"My baby!" shrieked Mrs Bodkin.

Now they could see Baby Joe,

sprawled on his back, looking rather confused and covered in snow while a walrus and a polar bear danced around him.

No wonder Joe looked confused. One moment he'd been playing with the buttons on the special TV remote, then – whoops – before he'd had time

to shout, he'd dropped the control and been sucked through the TV screen as if the glass was as soft as a rainbow. One moment he had been sitting on the warm carpet, looking at a winter wonderland on TV – and the next he was stranded on a block of ice, with snowflakes falling around him. The sky was black and the stars were shining.

Joe shivered, sat up and rubbed his head.

The walrus and the polar bear stopped dancing when they saw the little visitor. They bent down and peered at him.

"Hello, what's this?" said the walrus.

"It looks like a baby," said the polar bear, wiping the snow from his spectacles.

The walrus scratched his whiskers. "That's strange. He shouldn't be out alone in the cold. What are we going to do with him?"

“I don’t know,” said the polar bear.

“Can you see his mother anywhere?” asked the walrus.

“No.” The polar bear shook his head. “I can’t see anything in these glasses.”

They were quiet for a moment.

"Let's pretend it's not happening," suggested the walrus.

"Good idea!" said the polar bear.

And they walked away, arm in arm, for a mug of hot tea and a fried-egg sandwich.

Joe continued to sit on the ice with the snow gently drifting over his head. He wasn't dressed for the cold. His fingers were turning blue. His breath hung like steam in the frosty air.

"They've left him alone in the snow!" said Archie indignantly.

"What are you going to do to save him?" shouted Mrs Bodkin, glaring at her husband. She blamed Mr Bodkin for the accident.

"Switch off the TV!" shouted Mr Bodkin. "Pull out the plug! We'll soon stop this nonsense!" He was going to find his screwdriver set and take the television apart.

"No," cried Archie. "If we switch it off we might lose Baby Joe forever."

"That's right," said Mrs Bodkin. "How can you be so heartless?"

"Well, we can't stand here like lemons," grumbled Mr Bodkin.

"I think we should call Uncle Bernie," said Archie. And he hurried away to phone the Jackdaw's Nest.

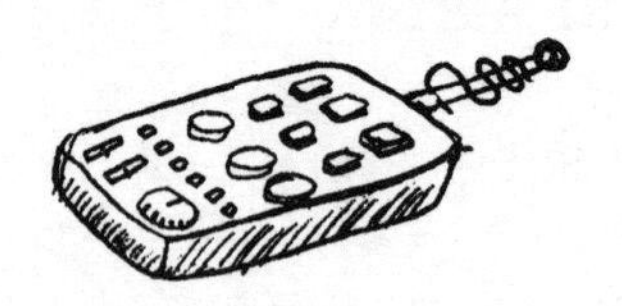

# Chapter 5

Uncle Bernie wasted no time in rushing back to the house. He stared at Baby Joe still trapped inside the TV set and then stared at the remote control left behind on the carpet.

He frowned and scratched his head. "I think he pressed 'Enter' by mistake," he said at last.

"Enter?" said Archie.

"Yes," said Uncle Bernie.

"Why would that make him enter the TV set?" asked Mr Bodkin. "It sounds very irregular to me."

"I don't know," said Uncle Bernie. "It's a mystery of science." He shook the remote control and heard a nasty rattle. "There must be something wrong with one of the connections."

"Well, what are you going to do to

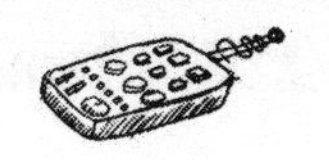

get our baby home again?" said Mrs Bodkin.

Uncle Bernie looked worried. He pressed a few buttons, hoping the problem would solve itself. Baby Joe grew large and then small and then went back to his normal size; he turned red and then green and then went back to his usual colour, but he was still on the wrong side of the television screen.

"I think we should try to move him into a different sort of programme," suggested Archie.

"What sort of programme?" asked Uncle Bernie.

"One without snow," said Archie.

"And how would that help?" demanded Mr Bodkin.

"At least he'd be warm and dry while we think about how to rescue him," explained Archie. He was eight years old and full of bright ideas.

"Quite right!" said Uncle Bernie. "We shouldn't leave him out in the cold."

"But how do we do it?" Mrs Bodkin wanted to know.

"We'll try the remote control again," said Archie. "Perhaps we can move Joe into a different programme when we press the buttons to change the channels."

"It might work!" said Uncle Bernie.

So Archie took the gadget and pressed the buttons. He was looking for his favourite show.

"There!" said Archie, as the television crackled and changed channels. "It's *Captain Marvellous in*

*Space*. You can always trust Captain Marvellous in an emergency."

They watched the screen. Captain Marvellous had been on a mission to the moon in six exciting episodes. Now he was getting ready to blast off to the stars in his Marvellous Galaxy Cruiser.

"Whoops – there goes Joe!" cried Mrs Bodkin as they saw their baby

appear at the top of the screen and then drop, with a thump, between the Captain's shiny space boots.

Joe sat up and blinked. He was still covered in snow. But when he saw Captain Marvellous, he smiled.

"Woo-woo!" he said to Captain Marvellous.

Marvellous hadn't seen the visitor – he was busy getting ready for another of his famous adventures.

"He'll be safe with the Captain while we try to come up with a rescue plan," said Archie confidently.

But moments before the Captain fired the rocket engines, he glanced down and saw the baby.

"Hello," he said. "How did you get here? We can't have babies blasting off into space. I'll leave you out for your mother."

He opened the hatch and placed Joe on the ground like an empty milk bottle on a doorstep.

Joe was so surprised that he didn't have

time to complain. When the rocket engines were fired he was blown into the air and found himself tumbling head over heels towards a deep and dusty crater.

"Stop!" shouted Mr Bodkin as Captain Marvellous shot off towards the stars. "You're leaving our baby boy on the moon."

He lost his temper and banged the TV with his fist.

"Getting angry won't save our baby from disappearing into a crater," Mrs Bodkin reminded him.

"Quick!" said Archie. "There's still time. I think we can save him by changing the programme."

He pressed another button on the remote control. The television crackled and changed channels.

"Don't put him with any wild animals," Mrs Bodkin warned her son as he started flicking through the

programmes again. "Be sure to choose something suitable. You never know what you'll find on TV."

"Who's that idiot?" said Uncle Bernie suddenly.

"That's Cyril the Magic Clown," said Archie as they stared at a man wearing red pantaloons and a pair of long rubber shoes.

Every afternoon, Cyril the Magic Clown performed hilarious conjuring tricks with the help of his lovely assistant, Janet. Sometimes he juggled with custard pies and sometimes he balanced a chair on his nose. Today he was planning to shoot strings of coloured handkerchiefs from the barrel of his magic cannon.

"Whoops – there goes Joe!" said Mrs Bodkin as they saw their baby appear at the top of the screen.

"He'll be safe with Cyril while we try to come up with a rescue plan," said Archie confidently. "He's Baby Joe's favourite character."

But Cyril hadn't seen Baby Joe. And when Baby Joe dropped into the show,

he dropped straight down the barrel of the magic cannon.

"Boo-hoo," he said in the dark. But his voice was muffled and no one heard him.

"Stop!" shouted Mr Bodkin at the TV set. "You can't shoot our baby from your magic cannon." He was still very angry and red in the face.

Cyril the Magic Clown struck a match and lit the fuse to fire the cannon while his lovely assistant played the trumpet and turned circles on silver roller skates.

"We'll never get him back again," sobbed Mrs Bodkin, wiping her eyes on her kitchen apron.

Archie looked at his father shouting and his mother sobbing and the fuse burning down in the cannon and he knew that he had to do something fast and he knew that he had to do something drastic.

"I have another idea," he said. "If I can follow Baby Joe into the TV set, I might be able to keep him safe and out of mischief."

"And how are you going to get

home again?" grumbled his father.

"I don't know," said Archie. "But Joe's too small to help himself and if we don't do something very soon that cannon will fire him through the ceiling."

"How are you going to get into the TV set?" asked his mother.

"Well, if I hold the remote control very tight and press 'Enter' . . ." said Archie hopefully.

"I don't recommend it," said Uncle Bernie.

"We don't know what will happen," said his mother.

"It might go wrong," said his father.

But it was too late. Before anyone could stop him, Archie had pointed the gadget at the TV and pressed the forbidden button.

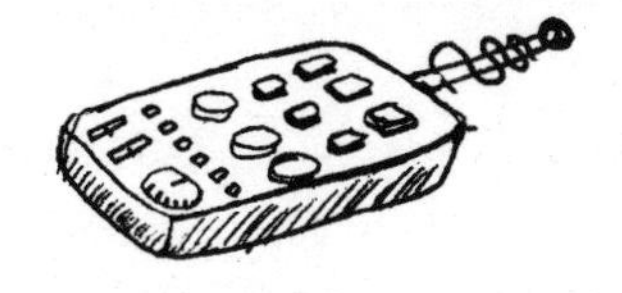

# Chapter 6

There was a crackle and a flash as Archie felt himself stretched and squeezed and lifted clean from the carpet. He was dragged forward in a loud whoosh and sucked through the

TV screen. It didn't hurt. It happened too quickly.

When he opened his eyes, Archie found himself standing on the stage behind Cyril's lovely assistant. The remote control was still clutched in his hand.

The lovely assistant looked surprised but, thinking Archie must be part of the act, she blew on her trumpet and skated around him in circles.

At that very moment there was a loud bang, a plume of fluttering

handkerchiefs and Baby Joe shot from the cannon.

Archie closed his eyes and threw out his hands. Baby Joe flew through the air . . . and dropped into Archie's arms. Archie was so surprised he'd caught him that he fell in a heap on the floor.

"Boo-boo," laughed Joe, and he blew a bubble. He was very pleased to see his big brother.

"Hello," said Archie when he'd recovered.

But Cyril the Clown looked angry. He blamed Archie for spoiling his trick.

"Hold tight," said Archie as he put Joe down, grabbed his hand and pressed the buttons on the remote control.

"Stop!" shouted Cyril.

The television crackled and changed channels as Cyril stamped towards them in his long rubber shoes . . . and vanished.

Archie and his baby brother found themselves tumbling slowly, head over heels, towards a sunlit ocean until they landed on the deck of a sailing ship. They could hear the waves splashing beneath them and canvas creaking above their heads as the wind caught in the sails.

"Whoops," said Archie as he sat up and rubbed his head. "This doesn't look very suitable. I think it's a pirate ship."

He was staring at a fierce-looking character with a black eyepatch and a ginger beard. He wore high boots and carried a cutlass in his belt.

"Stowaways!" roared the pirate captain when he saw Archie and Baby Joe. "We can't have stowaways

stealing the biscuits – we'll make them walk the plank!"

A fat pirate with silver earrings and gold teeth rushed forward and seized Archie and Joe by their collars. He bundled them to the end of the plank.

"Hold tight!" said Archie as he glanced down at the ocean beneath them. He squeezed Baby Joe's hand.

"We're leaving. We have to find someone sensible who is going to take us home."

"Jump!" shouted the pirate captain. "You're going overboard."

Archie pressed the buttons on the remote control.

The television crackled and changed channels as the fat pirate lunged forward to give Archie a nasty prod with his cutlass . . . and vanished.

Archie and his baby brother went tumbling head over heels until they found themselves slowly sinking towards dry land again. But now it was dark and the moon was shining. They could smell wood smoke and hear someone playing the harmonica.

"Whoops," said Archie as he sat up and looked around. "This doesn't look very helpful. I think we've landed in the Wild West."

He was staring at a circle of cowboys sitting around an open campfire. The cowboys had leather waistcoats and big moustaches. They

wore ten-gallon hats and carried six-shooters in their belts. They were busy cooking their supper when Archie and Joe dropped in on them.

"Rustlers!" growled one of the cowboys when he saw Archie and Baby Joe. He waved his fork in a threatening manner. "Catch them quick – they'll be trying to rustle our pork and beans."

The cowboys looked angry – they were obviously hungry. One of them jumped up and pulled a lasso from his saddlebag. He glared at Archie and Joe as he started to spin the rope, faster and faster, over his head.

"Hold tight!" said Archie as he saw the lasso flying towards them. He squeezed Baby Joe's hand. "We're leaving again."

"Gotcha!" shouted the cowboy as the lasso caught Archie and Joe in its noose.

Archie pressed the buttons on

the remote control.

The cowboy pulled hard on the rope, dragging Archie and Joe towards him.

The television crackled and changed channels as the cowboy made a grab for his captives . . . and vanished.

Archie and his baby brother went

tumbling head over heels until they found themselves at last sinking through a studio ceiling.

"This looks more promising," said Archie. There were lights and cameras and far below he could see a woman with big hair, who was reading the six o'clock TV news. She looked very sensible. She wore a blue jacket and dangly earrings.

She spoke about a politician who was worried about the price of

carrots, a film star who had written a book and a poodle winning first prize at a famous dog show.

"And that's the end of the news," she said.

She was just getting ready to read the weather report when Archie and Joe landed with a tremendous thump on her desk.

"Whoops – there they go!" said Uncle Bernie, still watching the giant TV screen in the Bodkins' living room.

Baby Joe sat up and sneezed. He looked dirty and lost and rather frightened. When he saw the woman with big hair he burst into tears.

"Boo-hoo!" he said to the woman.

The woman said nothing. She was meant to be forecasting rain, but when she saw the intruders she was so surprised that she clutched her throat as if she'd swallowed a tennis ball. Her dangly earrings started to tremble.

“I’m sorry,” said Archie politely. “We didn’t mean to frighten you.”

“I’ve had enough of this nonsense!” Mr Bodkin shouted at the TV set.

“Someone save my baby!” pleaded Mrs Bodkin.

And then, as they watched, a man with headphones dashed forward,

grabbed Archie and Joe from the newsdesk and hurried them from the picture.

"They've vanished," gasped Mr Bodkin.

"Where have they gone?" cried Mrs Bodkin.

"Don't ask me," said Uncle Bernie impatiently. "I don't know everything."

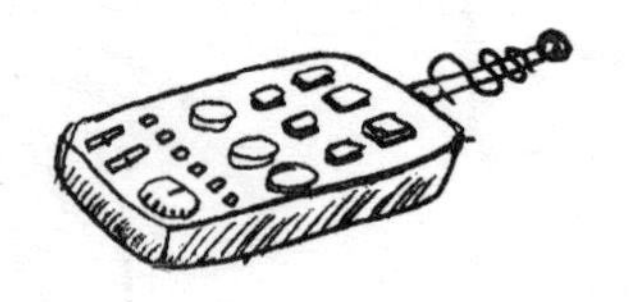

# Chapter 7

The man with headphones had taken Archie and Joe to the office of an important executive.

The important executive wanted to know what had happened to upset the

six o'clock news. It was a serious state of affairs.

Archie tried to explain how Baby Joe had got lost inside the TV set.

"That was very careless," said the important man.

"Yes," agreed Archie. "We'll be more careful in future. Now, I wonder if you could kindly put us in a taxi and send us home to 12 Hazelnut Avenue."

At seven o'clock that evening, a taxi stopped at 12 Hazelnut Avenue and the important man from the television studio rang the doorbell

and gave Archie and Joe back to their parents.

"Here is your baby," he said.

"Thank you," said Mrs Bodkin.

"And here's Archie," said the important man, "who deserves a medal for helping to save Baby Joe."

"We're very grateful. Thank you for bringing them home," said Mr Bodkin.

"Don't mention it," said the important man. "But please don't let it happen again. I'm very important. I have a large desk and several telephones. I don't have time to chase children."

"It won't happen again," promised Mrs Bodkin as she took Baby Joe away for a whoopsie, a wash and clean pyjamas.

"This is our fault," said Mr Bodkin

when the important man from the TV studio had gone. "We have only ourselves to blame. In future we must pick our programmes carefully and watch television as a family."

"That's very sensible," said Mrs Bodkin.

"And I think we had better return to watching our old TV," Archie told Uncle Bernie sadly. "I don't think your new invention was properly invented."

"You're probably right," said Uncle Bernie. "Perhaps there were too many grommets and gizmos."

Everyone agreed with him.

So they helped Uncle Bernie unplug his big contraption and take it back to the Jackdaw's Nest.

That evening the Bodkins sat together to watch their old TV from a

safe distance. They had hot chocolate and sultana biscuits.

While they watched, Mrs Bodkin took up her knitting, Mr Bodkin picked up the paper and started doing a crossword puzzle, and Archie looked through the pictures in his favourite caterpillar book.

"We're watching TV as a family,"

Archie told his baby brother.

But Joe – who was tired from his adventures – had already fallen asleep.

**The End**

*Also look out for*

# Little Archie and the Tongue-Tingling Super-Shrinking Powder

Turn the page to see
Little Archie in big trouble
once again . . .

# . . . Chapter 2

The trouble began on Archie's birthday. It was a Saturday. Archie woke up at the regular time and went downstairs to open his presents.

A birthday is an exciting event and Archie was hoping for surprises: a conjuring set or a junior detective kit containing interesting disguises.

But his mother gave him a fountain pen and a large bottle of ink.

"You can write me a thank-you letter," she said. His mother liked giving sensible presents.

Archie's father gave him a racing car, but the batteries weren't included.

"You can always pretend," said his father, and went into the garden to look at his cabbages.

His baby brother gave him a smile and did a whoopsie into the potty.

Archie felt a little disappointed.

It was late when Uncle Bernie arrived. He brought Archie a present wrapped in a piece of blue waxed paper and tied with a length of hairy string. Archie grinned. He knew it must be something exciting. He gave it a sniff and held it against his ear.

"Open it," said Uncle Bernie.

So Archie untied the string and discovered a small glass bottle filled with a yellow powder that glittered when he gave it a shake.

"It's Magic Shrinking Powder," Uncle Bernie said . . .

Read the book to find out what tongue-tingling trouble comes next!

## A selected list of titles available from Macmillan Children's Books

The prices shown below are correct at the time of going to press. However, Macmillan Publishers reserves the right to show new retail prices on covers, which may differ from those previously advertised.

---

| | | |
|---|---|---|
| **Miles Gibson and Neal Layton** | | |
| Little Archie and the Tongue-Tingling Super-Shrinking Powder | 978-0-330-44189-6 | £3.99 |
| **Martine Murray** | | |
| Henrietta (there's no one better) | 978-0-330-43958-9 | £3.99 |
| Henrietta (the great go-getter) | 978-0-230-52884-0 | £6.99 |
| **Pirate Stories** | 978-0-330-45148-2 | £4.99 |
| Stories chosen by Emma Young | | |

---

All Pan Macmillan titles can be ordered from our website, www.panmacmillan.com, or from your local bookshop and are also available by post from:

**Bookpost, PO Box 29, Douglas, Isle of Man IM99 1BQ**

Credit cards accepted. For details:
Telephone: 01624 677237
Fax: 01624 670923
Email: bookshop@enterprise.net
www.bookpost.co.uk

**Free postage and packing in the United Kingdom**